Fearless Freddy

by Rika Summers
illustrated by Marc Mongeau

Harcourt
SCHOOL PUBLISHERS

Requests for permission to make copies of any part of the work should be addressed to School Permissions and Copyrights, Harcourt, Inc., 6277 Sea Harbor Drive, Orlando, Florida 32887-6777. Fax: 407-345-2418.

HARCOURT and the Harcourt Logo are trademarks of Harcourt, Inc., registered in the United States of America and/or other jurisdictions.

Printed in China

ISBN 10: 0-15-350500-1
ISBN 13: 978-0-15-350500-3

Ordering Options
ISBN 10: 0-15-350333-5 (Grade 3 Below-Level Collection)
ISBN 13: 978-0-15-350333-7 (Grade 3 Below-Level Collection)
ISBN 10: 0-15-357487-9 (package of 5)
ISBN 13: 978-0-15-357487-0 (package of 5)

2 3 4 5 6 7 8 9 10 985 12 11 10 09 08 07

Once there was a brave little dog who had no home. Freddy lived as best as he could. He watched out for cars, he avoided buses, and he found places to sleep.

He roamed around the city to find food. Sometimes he received decent scraps from people. Sometimes he found meals in trash cans. Sometimes he ate nothing at all.

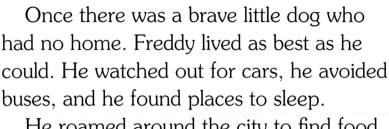

Life was often difficult, but Freddy was not afraid. He could take care of himself because he knew the city well.

One day, Freddy wandered by a junkyard. He noticed that the gate was open a bit. Inside the yard, beside a doghouse, there were several bowls of food!

CARL

Freddy hadn't eaten for hours, so he thought hard. Should he take some of the food? A dog came out of its house and smiled at Freddy.

"Come on in, fellow," he said. "That is, if you've a fondness for a tasty meal."

The dog's name was Carl. Freddy
and Carl became good friends. Carl was
the only dog who really belonged in the
junkyard. Carl felt very sorry for dogs that
did not have homes and let them stay.
Freddy became friends with these dogs too.

One day, Mort asked Freddy, "Where do you sleep? When the junkyard closes, you always leave."

"I sleep wherever it is warm and dry," replied Freddy.

Mort looked surprised and asked, "Why not stay here?"

"I can stay here?" Freddy asked.

"Of course, you can, you ridiculous hound," laughed Mort.

"We sleep in old cars where it is warm and dry," Mort said. "Nobody bothers us, and Carl shares his food. What could be better?"

Freddy was filled with emotion when he heard this. He decided to stay.

Freddy had finally found a home. He
ate good food instead of disgraceful trash.
There were no more rushing cars, and rain
never poured down upon him.

"I couldn't be happier," Freddy thought,
"if I were to inherit a kingdom."

Freddy did not stay inside the junkyard
all the time. He still liked to go out and see
the world.

Every night, though, Freddy went back to
the junkyard and his friends. When winter
came, they would crawl into one of the old
cars and curl up together to stay warm.

Then, early one morning as the dogs slept in a car, there was a problem! Freddy woke up first. Something didn't feel right. The car was moving! This car hadn't run in years. What was happening? Freddy looked out at the yard. A machine was picking up the car! Freddy yelped an alarm. This must be a mistake!

The dogs leaped out of the car as it left the ground. Quickly Freddy counted his friends. Mort was missing! He must still be inside the car! The car was high above the ground now.

"I must help Mort," Freddy thought.

Freddy charged the machine. He barked
as loudly as he could. He pretended to
attack it. He ran around it. He danced in
front of it.

Finally, the workers stopped the machine to keep from hitting Freddy. They brought the car back to the ground. They laughed when Mort spilled out.

"What a brave dog!" they said of Freddy.

"Thank you, friend Freddy," said Mort.

"Thanks, fearless Freddy," Carl grinned.

Later the workers shared their lunches with the happy dogs.

Think Critically

1. How would you describe Freddy?

2. How is Freddy's life different after he comes to live in the junkyard?

3. What did Freddy do to save his friend Mort?

4. Why do you think Freddy still likes to roam around the city?

5. What character in the story was your favorite? Why?

 Social Studies

Explore a City Freddy loved to explore the city where he lived. Choose a city that you have heard about. Look in a book or on the Internet to find out about this city. Then write five facts about the city.

 School-Home Connection Tell friends and family members this story. What are their favorite parts?